Printed in the U.S.A.

ISBN 0-7172-8287-2

JIM HENSON'S MUPPETS IN

Show-and-Yell

A Book About Manners

By Richard Chevat • Illustrated by Joe Ewers

GROLIER

It was bright and early in the morning, and Gonzo was the first one out of bed.

"Oh, boy!" he said to his toy chicken, Camilla. "Today is show-and-tell at school, and I get to bring in my pet rock. I can hardly wait!"

Gonzo jumped up and ran to his dresser. There was the box where his pet rock lived.

"Hi, Cornelius," Gonzo said to the smooth, gray rock. "Let's practice your trick."

Gonzo put Cornelius on the floor. "Stay, Cornelius!" he commanded. Cornelius didn't move. "Good rock," Gonzo said happily. "Boy, I can't wait to show you off."

Just then, Gonzo heard his grandmother calling from the hallway. "Don't forget to brush your teeth," she said.

"Okay!" Gonzo called, and rushed to the bathroom in his pajamas. At the bathroom door, he bumped into his cousin Gander, who was also on his way in to brush his teeth.

"Out of the way, Gander," Gonzo said, and pushed right by him. "I can't be late. I'm taking Cornelius to school today."

"Hey," Gander shouted as Gonzo closed the bathroom door in his face. "I was here first!"

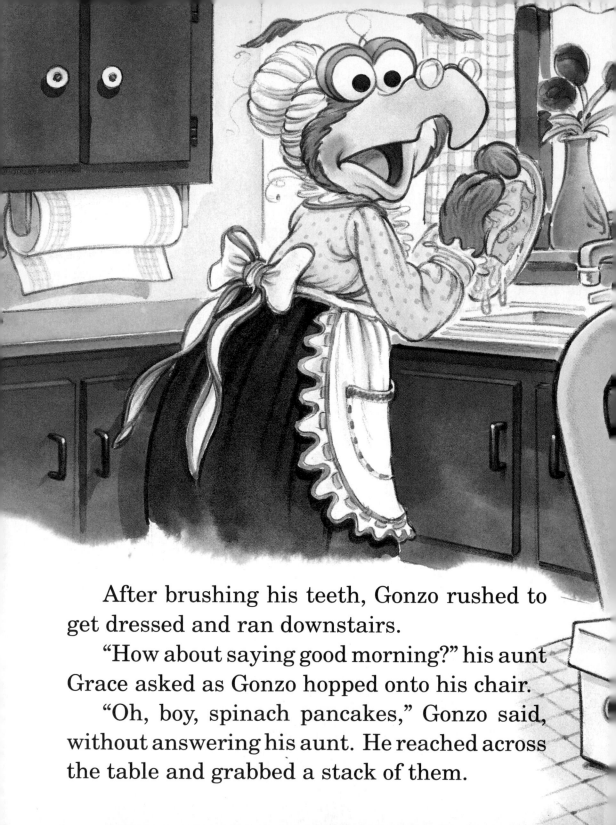

After brushing his teeth, Gonzo rushed to
get dressed and ran downstairs.

"How about saying good morning?" his aunt
Grace asked as Gonzo hopped onto his chair.

"Oh, boy, spinach pancakes," Gonzo said,
without answering his aunt. He reached across
the table and grabbed a stack of them.

"Gonzo, where are your manners?" asked his grandmother. "Those pancakes were for Aunt Grace."

"I've got to get to the bus on time," said Gonzo, his mouth full of pancakes. "Today is show-and-tell."

When Gonzo got to the bus stop, some of the other kids were already there.

"I'm bringing my pet rock to show-and-tell," Gonzo told Rowlf excitedly.

"I'm bringing my electric keyboard," said Rowlf, but Gonzo wasn't listening.

Just then, the big, yellow school bus pulled up to the curb. Gonzo pushed ahead of everyone and ran for a seat.

"How rude," Piggy sniffed as she walked past Gonzo and sat behind him. "Don't you know you're supposed to wait in line?"

"Cornelius needs a window seat," Gonzo explained. "Otherwise, he gets bus sick."

In class, Gonzo was so excited that he could barely stay in his seat. He kept asking Mr. Bumper if it was time for show-and-tell. Gonzo even interrupted Mr. Bumper while he was reading Gonzo's favorite story, "The Chicken Who Saved the Universe."

"When is show-and-tell?" he called out.

"Not until later," Mr. Bumper said. "Now, don't call out, Gonzo. You know it's not polite."

Finally, show-and-tell time arrived. First it was Rowlf's turn. Then Fozzie got up to talk.

"My grandfather Ozzie gave me this whoopee cushion," Fozzie began.

"I have my pet rock," Gonzo called out. He just couldn't help himself.

"Hey, wait your turn," said Fozzie.

"Yeah," said Rowlf. "This is show-and-tell, not show-and-yell."

"Okay, Gonzo, it's your turn," said Mr. Bumper when Fozzie was done.

Gonzo ran up to the front of the room. "This is Cornelius," he said in a rush, holding his rock up for everyone to see. "I found him one day in the park, and he followed me home. Well, he didn't exactly follow me, because he's a rock."

Gonzo talked about Cornelius for a long time. Then show-and-tell was over. Everyone went out to the schoolyard to play. Gonzo ran over to where Piggy was jumping rope with Rowlf and Kermit.

"Hey, Piggy!" Gonzo shouted. "Did you see Cornelius? Isn't he neat?"

"Gonzo!" Piggy moaned, and stopped jumping. "You made me lose count. Even that silly rock has better manners than you!"

That night during supper, Gonzo told his family what had happened at school.

"Everyone just got mad at me," he said.

"I'm sorry your show-and-tell didn't go well," said Grandma kindly. "But maybe you were so excited today, you forgot to have good manners. Maybe if you—"

"What difference does that make?" Gonzo said, interrupting his grandmother. He reached across the table and took the last helping of carrot-olive loaf.

"Gonzo," said Aunt Grace. "How would you like it if no one had any manners at all?"

"I wouldn't care," said Gonzo. "It might even be fun."

Gonzo kept talking about show-and-tell right up until bedtime. He was so busy thinking about it that he didn't even answer Gander when he said, "Good night, Gonzo."

"Sleep tight, little Gonzo," said Grandma as she tucked him in. "You've had a busy day."

"Hmm," Gonzo grumbled, and he fell asleep still thinking about show-and-tell.

Suddenly, Gonzo found himself on the floor of his room.

"Who pushed me?" he asked, blinking.

"I did," said Camilla, his toy chicken. "I wanted more room in the bed."

"Well, you could have asked," said Gonzo. Then he frowned. *That's funny,* he thought. *Camilla never talked before.*

Sleepily, Gonzo went to the bathroom to brush his teeth. He was at the door when Gander brushed right past him and closed the door in his face.

"Hey, no fair!" Gonzo started to say, but then he heard his grandmother calling from downstairs.

"Hurry up, Gonzo. Breakfast is almost gone!"

Gonzo rushed to get dressed without even brushing his teeth. But by the time he got to the kitchen, there were no more anchovy omelets left.

"You didn't save me any," he complained, but Grandma didn't answer.

"Hurry. You'll miss your bus," she said as she pushed him out the door.

Gonzo ran all the way to the bus stop. He was the first kid there.

At least I'll get a window seat! he thought.

Then, just as the bus arrived, Piggy, Rowlf, and all the other kids ran up.

"Get out of the way!" they yelled as they pushed Gonzo to the side. Gonzo tried to follow.

"Sorry, no room," said the bus driver. "You'll have to walk."

Things were even worse at school.

Every time Gonzo tried to answer a question, Kermit or one of the other kids interrupted him. And when Gonzo went to get some crayons from the art cabinet, Mr. Bumper ran in front of him and took the last box!

"What's happening?" shouted Gonzo. "Why doesn't anyone have any manners?"

"I thought you didn't care about manners," said Mr. Bumper.

"No," said Gonzo. "I like manners!"

"No manners!" shouted all the children.

"Gonzo! Gonzo! Wake up!" someone called.

Gonzo rubbed his eyes and looked around. He was back in his bed, and there was his grandmother, shaking him awake.

"You were having a bad dream," she said gently.

"It was terrible!" Gonzo said, sitting up in bed. "No one had any manners at all. Everyone pushed and shoved and no one said please—not even Mr. Bumper."

"It was just a dream," Grandma said, smiling.

"I'm sure glad," Gonzo replied. "I'd hate it if no one had any manners."

"Glad to hear it," said Grandma. "Now, go back to sleep. Would you like Cornelius to keep you company?"

"Yes, please," answered Gonzo as his grandmother brought his pet rock from the dresser. "And Grandma?"

"Yes, Gonzo?" Grandma asked.

"Thank you," said Gonzo. And he lay down and went back to sleep.

Let's Talk About Manners

Gonzo was so excited about bringing his pet rock to school for show-and-tell that he forgot his manners. Later, he had a bad dream in which everyone *else* forgot their manners, too...and it wasn't any fun at all.

Here are some questions about manners for you to think about:

Have you ever been so excited about something that you forgot your manners? What happened?

Why do you think it's important for people to have manners?